The Adventures of
Goo Goo Malou

Written and Illustrated by
Ron Mescall

This Book Belongs To:

_____

Order this book online at www.trafford.com
or email orders@trafford.com

Most Trafford titles are also available at major online book retailers.

 www.trafford.com

North America & international
toll-free: 844 688 6899 (USA & Canada)
fax: 812 355 4082

Our mission is to efficiently provide the world's finest, most comprehensive book publishing service, enabling every author to experience success. To find out how to publish your book, your way, and have it available worldwide, visit us online at www.trafford.com

Because of the dynamic nature of the Internet, any web addresses or links contained in this book may have changed since publication and may no longer be valid. The views expressed in this work are solely those of the author and do not necessarily reflect the views of the publisher, and the publisher hereby disclaims any responsibility for them.

Any people depicted in stock imagery provided by Getty Images are models, and such images are being used for illustrative purposes only.
Certain stock imagery © Getty Images.

ISBN: 978-1-6987-0923-9 (sc)
ISBN: 978-1-6987-0922-2 (e)

Print information available on the last page.

Trafford rev. 09/25/2021

My name is Goo Goo Malou,
a very magic caterpillar too.
Someday I may fly away,
but in the land of Nowhere Somewhere
I spend each day.

My home is no special place in town,
only under the leaves and all around.
I think I'm special as many say
because I'm happy all the day.

The sunshine makes me feel so good.
But if I could fly--Oh if I could,
I'd soar the flowers up and down
and over the hills and all around.
I'm looking for a special home filled
with happiness that I can spin,
and hoping that many friends I can win.
Perhaps I will meet one friend or even many.
I only hope she's like my Lady Bug Penny.

She is so warm, kind and quick.
Last time I saw her she was on a stick.
Her bright color shown through a vein of light
as I watched her soar in constant flight.
Oh my Lady Bug so fair, I need a home.
Do you know where?
"I'm glad to see you Goo Goo young friend.
Of all my thinking I shall lend...

"I'll help you find a home to spin my dear,
and learn some of the values you will hear.
We'll travel down the hollow and through the weeds
and you will meet flowers that do good deeds.
They talk and even sing all day
and they will teach you life's values along the way.
I'm Lady Bug Penny and that is true
and I will teach you, Goo Goo Malou.
Soon we'll also meet Edison Randall,
a lightening bug--who lights up like a candle!

"It's time to travel Goo Goo my dear
because Edison Randall Bug is near.
Today we travel over field and stream
to a place to spin our life's dream.
Remember, it's important to dream everyday
and leave your troubles along the way.
Oh Edison Randall, our lightening bug friend,
he's coming just around the bend.
Edison Bug--he is so near.
He will teach you COURAGE and stop your fear.

"It's time to leave you,
Goo Goo my dear.
I hear the Angel Bug is near.
I'm as old as a lady bug can be
and I have traveled over land and sea.
I'll join the lady bugs in heaven's sky;
But of you my memories will never die."

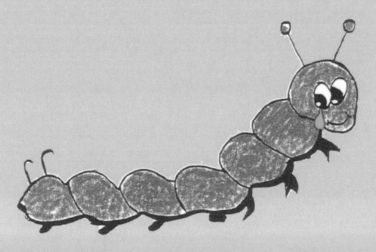

Great moments have been between us, Lady Bug Penny.
As I leave you to go on adventures many.
I promise to learn those important skills and really try
even if leaving you makes me cry.

"Goo Goo Malou, I want to teach you
about courage today.
Take this important value on your way.
I flit through the stars and sometimes the night.
I used to be frail
until I got a little lightning tail!

Know your fears and discuss them many
to me and to your friend, Lady Bug Penny.
It's no disgrace to experience fear in your life
as you face everyday strife.
We will approach FEAR together as we go on a walk
to overcome fear, it's important to talk.

COURAGE

PARENTS:

1. To help your child identify their fears, ask questions and explore the reasons behind behavior.

2. Praise the child's courage to face physical fear--for example a dark room, a dog, a bird, an insect.

3. Naming the child's fear is the first step--talk about it.

4. Courage is having heart--it's no disgrace to experience fear. It's a normal feeling.

5. Courage does not mean the absence of fear.

6. Approach fear together--name it and discuss it.

7. Always talk realistically about the matter of bereavement or physical limits.

8. Hug your child.

Courage is the mental or moral strength to withstand danger or fear

FRIENDSHIP

Dear Magic Caterpillar my friend,
your magic will last until the end.
Now I must leave you at The Gate of Flowers
where life's values soar just like towers.
Enter this land and spin a home
and remember Friend, you are never alone.
Our friendship will last throughout all your stages
and my heart will be with you throughout the ages.
It's time to go, and best wishes I'll lend
because my caterpillar, you are my friend!

The Gate of Flowers

PARENTS:

1. Begin by a model of friendship.

2. Express what real friends are.

3. Discuss helping each other as friendship grows.

4. Demonstrate that friendship includes communication, advice, praise, loyalty, and trust.

5. Discuss feelings for various people and family.

6. Friendship involves both giving and receiving.

7. You are your child's sanctuary from those who reject their friendship.

8. Talk about your child's friends and peers.

9. Hug your child.

RESPECT

Be kind to everyone you meet each day
and you will find kindness along the way.
Do the best with your good deeds
and you will not become bad weeds.

The Land of Flowers

PARENTS:

1. Self-esteem will protect your child from unhealthy relationships, alcohol, smoking and delinquency.
2. Recognize and explore your child's unique talents and relationships.
3. Be positive. Give reinforcement. Spend time together developing skills.
4. Make them feel part of decision making.
5. Accept the good and bad. Build self-esteem to have them accept themselves.
6. Hug your child.

SELF-ESTEEM

Do something good for someone each day
and you'll build your self-esteem along the way

The Happy Talking Flowers

HONESTY

You should be honest each and every day
as you follow your heart along the way.

The Truthful Flowers

Life is better when you try
and it's alright to sometimes cry.
Remember you're special, and life can be gold
even when you start to grow old.
Life is a real adventure of sort
when you add love in your heart.
Feelings are special when you see the light
and think of things that are lovely and right.
Dwell on the fine and good things everyday
and many right values will come your way.

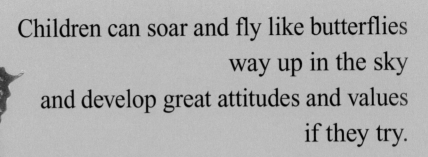

Children can soar and fly like butterflies
way up in the sky
and develop great attitudes and values
if they try.

I'm a magic butterfly and that's no lie.
Come with me and watch me fly.
I have great values everyday
that I have learned along the way.
We all can learn and soar the sky
and develop great attitudes if we try.
I can fly as high as any
remembering Edison and Lady Bug Penny.
Life's a great adventure if you dwell on the good things we know.
So now it's time for me to go,
up in the clouds and out of sight.
...And wishing you all a warm Good Night.

Respect for others will help build
meaningful relationships.

1. Lead by example. Avoid raising your voice, even if
   you feel frustrated.

2. Apologize to your child if you feel like you were
   exceptionally harsh on him or her.

3. Talk to your child and work out ways to avoid
   arguments in the future.

4. Thank people who help you, and it will reinforce
   that your child do the same. Nudge him or her
   gently before you say "Thank you" or "You're
   welcome" so they notice.

5. Become involved in the community, and bring
   your child with you.

6. Teach your child to respect other people's property
   as if it were their own. This will help when
   borrowing and lending toys with their friends. It
   will also help with cooperation in the future.

It's healthy for your child to feel good
about themselves.

1. Self-esteem will protect your child from forming
    unhealthy relationships. Talk and spend time with
    your child.

2. Recognize your child's unique skills and talents.
    Most important, support them. Your child will be
    less likely to abuse drugs or alcohol in the future if
    they feel they have something better to do with
    their time.

3. Let your child make decisions sometimes. Even
    something as simple as deciding what to eat for
    dinner will give your child a sense of responsibility
    and participation in your family.

4. Accept the good and the bad. Keep in touch with
    your child if you think something is bothering them.
    This will remind them that their happiness is
    important to you.

6. Hug your child, especially when you think he or she
    is having a bad day.

Your child should be comfortable
with being honest.

1. Set an example for your child by following through
    with *your* promises and plans.

2. If your child witnesses you telling a lie, do not try
    to justify it to make yourself feel better. Tell them
    that you were wrong. It lets them know that even
    adults make mistakes. It also lets your children
    feel closer to you, and know it's okay to admit when
    they are wrong as well.

3. Teach your chid how sharing, borrowing, and lending
    toys with their friends is good. Also teach them that
    borrowing without asking, stealing, or hiding toys
    from siblings or classmates is wrong.

Courage will help your child be more
confident in all aspects of their lives.

1. Identify your child's fears by talking about them.
   Also explore why they might have those fears.

2. Share your fears so that your child knows it's okay
   to sometimes be afraid.

3. Tell your child that courage means confronting their
   fears; it doesn't always mean getting rid of them.

4. Help your child think through ways to confront their
   problems. Two heads are better than one.

5. Praise your child's courage and decision to face
   their fears.

THE SINGLE BIGGEST PREDICTION OF HIGH
ACADEMIC AND HIGH ACT SCORES IS READING TO
CHILDREN. NOT FLASH CARDS, NOT WORKBOOKS,
NOT FANCY PRESCHOOLS BUT MOM AND DAD
TAKING TIME EVERY DAY OR NIGHT (OR BOTH)
TO SIT AND READ THEM GREAT BOOKS.

I PLEDGE ALLEGIANCE TO THE FLAG OF THE UNITED STATES OF AMERICA AND TO THE REPUBLIC FOR WHICH IT STANDS ONE NATION UNDER GOD INDIVISIBLE WITH LIBERTY AND JUSTICE FOR ALL.

Printed in the United States
by Baker & Taylor Publisher Services